The Case Of The ICY IGLOO INN

Look for more great books in

The New Adventures of MARY-KATE & ASHLEY™ series:

The Case Of The Great Elephant Escape
The Case Of The Summer Camp Caper
The Case Of The Surfing Secret
The Case Of The Green Ghost
The Case Of The Big Scare Mountain Mystery
The Case Of The Slam Dunk Mystery
The Case Of The Rock Star's Secret
The Case Of The Cheerleading Camp Mystery
The Case Of The Flying Phantom
The Case Of The Creepy Castle
The Case Of The Golden Slipper
The Case Of The Flapper 'Napper
The Case Of The High Seas Secret
The Case Of The Logical I Ranch
The Case Of The Dog Camp Mystery
The Case Of The Screaming Scarecrow
The Case Of The Jingle Bell Jinx
The Case Of The Game Show Mystery
The Case Of The Mall Mystery
The Case Of The Weird Science Mystery
The Case Of Camp Crooked Lake
The Case Of The Giggling Ghost
The Case Of The Candy Cane Clue
The Case Of The Hollywood Who-Done-It
The Case Of The Sundae Surprise
The Case Of Clue's Circus Caper
The Case Of Camp Pom-Pom
The Case Of The Tattooed Cat
The Case Of The Nutcracker Ballet
The Case Of The Clue At The Zoo
The Case Of The Easter Egg Race
The Case Of The Dog Show Mystery
The Case Of The Cheerleading Tattletale
The Case Of The Haunted Maze
The Case Of The Hidden Holiday Riddle

and coming soon
The Case Of The Unicorn Mystery

The Case Of The
ICY IGLOO INN

by Judy Katschke

HarperEntertainment
An Imprint of HarperCollins*Publishers*

A PARACHUTE PRESS BOOK

Parachute Publishing, L.L.C.
156 Fifth Avenue
New York, NY 10010

Dualstar Publications
1801 Century Park East
12th Floor
Los Angeles, CA 90067

HarperEntertainment
An Imprint of HarperCollins*Publishers*
10 East 53rd Street, New York, NY 10022

For information address HarperCollins Publishers Inc.,
10 East 53rd Street, New York, NY 10022.

ISBN 0-06-059595-7

First printing: January 2005

Printed in the United States of America

www.mary-kateandashley.com

10 9 8 7 6 5 4 3 2 1

1

WAY TO SNOW!

"Wow!" my sister, Ashley, said. "You don't see snow like *this* at home in California!"

"Unless it's in a snow globe!" I joked.

Ashley and I still couldn't believe it. It was winter break, and we were sitting in a dogsled pulled by a team of Siberian huskies. And here's the best part—we were heading straight for a hotel made of *ice*!

"You girls are going to love the Icy Igloo Inn!" Irving Cathcart called from the back as he steered the sled. "As Iris and I like to say, 'It's where cool rules!'"

Irving and his wife Iris live all the way up in northern Canada, where they run the Icy Igloo Inn. Irving is our great-grandma Olive's first cousin.

Ashley and I think Great-grandma Olive is the best great-grandma in the world. She's also the world's best detective! She always talks about the inn and now we finally get to see it.

"Iris and I heard that you girls are detectives too," Irving told us. "Is that true?"

I nodded. "Ashley and I run the Olsen and Olsen Detective Agency from the attic of our house," I said.

"Some people call us the Trenchcoat Twins," Ashley explained with a little shiver. "But it's way too cold for just trenchcoats out here!"

The dogs kicked up snow as they raced on. Our sled passed frozen lakes and snow-

frosted trees. I suddenly spotted a big white building in the distance. It looked all white and shiny, like a vanilla popsicle!

"Wow!" I exclaimed. "That house is totally covered with snow!"

"That's because it *is* snow . . . and ice!" Irving said. "Girls, welcome to the Icy Igloo Inn!"

My mouth dropped open. So did Ashley's. We thought the inn would look like a giant igloo—the kind that Eskimos build. Instead, the inn looked like a big cottage with a pointy roof. Everything seemed to be made of ice—even the front door and the shutters on the windows!

"The inn melts every spring, and we build it again every winter," Iris explained.

"Awesome!" I cried.

The huskies stopped in front of the inn. Irving helped us climb out of the sled. Then he held open the front door of the ice hotel as we walked inside. It was so cold, we could see our breath hanging in the air like little white clouds.

Ashley and I looked around and gasped. The walls were made of solid ice too. Luckily the floors were made of hard-packed snow, so we didn't need ice skates!

"There you are!" a voice called out.

Ashley and I turned. A woman with rosy cheeks and bright blue eyes hurried toward us. She wore a blue parka, furry white boots, and a hat with earflaps.

"Here comes Iris with a warm welcome!" Irving said.

"Not *too* warm, Irving!" Iris said, wagging a gloved finger. "Or the inn might melt!"

The Cathcarts showed us around the Icy Igloo Inn. There was a central living room, a dining room, lots of bedrooms, and a kitchen for preparing food. And all the furniture was carved out of—you guessed it—ice!

There was even an ice-cream parlor with a counter and stools made of ice. But

instead of ice cream, Irving and Iris served sno-cones made of real snow!

"Are the sno-cone cups made of snow too?" Ashley asked.

"No, dear," Iris said. "Not *everything* in the inn is made of ice or snow."

"In fact, there's a heated bathhouse attached to the hotel," Irving told us.

"Good!" I chuckled. The thought of an ice-cube shower made me shiver!

Next the Cathcarts showed us to our bedroom. Inside was an ice chair carved to look like a big seashell. And a beautiful night table carved out of ice too. Spread out on the beds were two thick fur rugs.

"Those are reindeer skins," Iris explained. "They're great for keeping you warm during the night."

"Cool," I said.

"You mean *cold*!" Ashley said. She rubbed her mittens together. "Where do you keep the heaters?"

"Heaters?" Irving and Iris cried together.

"We don't allow anything that might melt the inn before the spring thaw," Iris said. "No hot plates, no hair dryers—"

"And no salt either," Irving added. "Salt melts ice."

"What about hot cocoa?" I asked. "What's a winter vacation without hot cocoa and marshmallows?"

"We allow *some* hot food and drinks at the inn," Irving said. "Like hot cocoa and soup."

"Just try not to spill any," Iris said in a shaky voice. "You have no idea what spilled cocoa can do to ice!"

"Now follow us, girls," Irving said with a smile. "There's someone I want you to meet."

As we followed the Cathcarts out of the room, I whispered to Ashley, "They're really nervous that the inn might melt."

"Yeah," Ashley whispered. "Great-grandma Olive didn't tell us that!"

The Cathcarts led us to a room we hadn't

seen yet. The first thing I noticed was an icy chandelier hanging from the ceiling. The next thing I noticed was a bunch of sculptures carved out of ice.

A boy with blond hair stepped out from behind one. He was wearing a black parka, black pants, and black boots.

"This is Lars Lindstrom," Iris said. "He's only fourteen years old, and he carved all these sculptures. He's the champion junior ice sculptor of his country."

"Of the *world*!" Lars corrected.

"Lars is visiting from Sweden," Irving added. "His parents are old friends of ours."

"And he's staying here from Wednesday until Sunday, just like you girls," Iris explained. "Then he's leaving us his sculptures for our future guests to enjoy."

"These sculptures rock!" I said as we checked them out. Lars had carved an oversize penny, a huge bottle cap, and even a giant toad!

"I call this group of sculptures *Inside My Little Brother's Pocket*," Lars said.

"Lars!" Iris gasped. She pointed to his chest. "Is that a camera around your neck?"

"Yes," Lars said. "Why?"

"Flash photography is not allowed at the inn," Irving said. "The heat from the flash might melt the ice!"

Is he joking? I wondered.

"Nonsense!" Lars said. "I *must* photograph the inn."

"Why?" Iris asked.

Lars didn't answer.

The Cathcarts exchanged worried glances. Then they shook their heads at Lars.

"Sorry, Lars," Irving said. "But if you insist on taking pictures, you'll have to leave the Icy Igloo Inn."

Lars turned away. "Nobody asks Lars Lindstrom to leave," he said under his breath. "From *anywhere*!"

"This is what I call a 'heated discussion'!" I whispered to Ashley.

"Don't let them hear you say *heat*!" Ashley giggled.

Ashley and I went to explore the inn on our own. We checked out the ice bookshelves in the living room. They were filled with real books.

"Hey, Ashley," I said. "Did you notice that Iris and Irving both have the initials *I.C.*? As in . . . *icy*?"

Ashley was busy rubbing a frosty windowpane with one mitten. "Check out this awesome view, Mary-Kate!" she said.

I looked out the window. A frozen lake was surrounded by snow-dusted trees.

"It's a winter wonderland!" I declared.

Then suddenly . . . *Splash!*

We stared out the window. A man and a woman were bobbing in the freezing lake!

"Omigosh, Mary-Kate!" Ashley cried. "Those people just fell through the ice!"

2

COLD CASE

"We have to save them, Ashley!" I cried.

My sister and I raced to the front door. I leaned out and shouted, "Don't worry! We're going to get help!"

The man and the woman stopped bobbing. They turned toward us and smiled.

"What for?" the woman asked.

"Come on in!" the man shouted. "The water's fine!"

What? Ashley and I walked slowly outside. We stared at the couple in the freezing water.

"Are they swimming?" I asked.

"You got that right," a voice said.

Ashley and I whirled around. Standing behind us was a sandy-haired boy who was about eleven years old. He was wearing a bright yellow parka, sunglasses, and a neon-green cap. He was wearing boots, but his legs were bare below his bright Hawaiian board shorts!

"I'm Kevin Douglas," he said. "That's my mom and dad in the water."

"Why are they swimming in ice water?" Ashley asked.

"Because they're Polar Bears," Kevin said.

"Polar bears?" I asked. I stared at the couple splashing in the icy water. "They look pretty human to me."

"No!" Kevin laughed. "My mom and dad are members of the Polar Bear Club. They like swimming in cold water in the winter."

"Brrr!" Ashley shivered.

"I'm Mary-Kate Olsen, and this is my

sister, Ashley," I said. "Were you about to go for a swim too?"

Kevin shook his head. "Ice water isn't my thing," he said. "I'm a surfer dude!"

"Then you must be from California, like us," I said. "Or from Hawaii or Florida."

"I wish!" Kevin groaned. "We're from Minnesota, which is cold enough. But every year we come to the Icy Igloo Inn so my mom and dad can go ice swimming. I haven't been to a warm, sunny beach my whole life!"

"So you've never actually surfed?" I asked.

"Never!" Kevin said. "This place is cool, but I wish we could leave early. Then we could go to a beach and I could finally catch the perfect wave."

Ashley pointed to Kevin's shorts. "The only thing you're going to 'catch' dressed like that," she said, "is a cold!"

The Cathcarts walked outside with Lars. He wasn't wearing his camera anymore.

They must have settled the argument, I thought.

Two more people came out of the inn. One was a red-haired woman dressed in a sheepskin coat and leather boots. She had her arm around a red-haired girl who looked about twelve. The girl was dressed in a light blue furry jacket and a matching hat. In her arms was a tiny Chihuahua. The little dog was also wearing a furry blue coat. And matching doggy earmuffs!

"Mary-Kate," Ashley whispered. "Isn't that—"

"I think so!" I said. I turned to the girl and asked, "Aren't you Dakota Valencia? The child supermodel?"

The girl looked bored as she nodded.

"I used to be a supermodel when I was a girl!" the older woman piped up. "You might recognize me. I'm Jade Valencia. I was on the cover of *Seventeen* magazine! And *Fourteen*, *Fifteen*, and *Sixteen* too!" she joked.

"Mo-om!" Dakota groaned.

Ashley reached out to pet the Chihuahua. "That's a really cute dog," she said. "What's his name?"

"It's Brutus," Dakota said.

"Ashley and I have a dog too," I said. "She's a basset hound named Clue."

"As in . . . *clueless*?" Dakota asked.

"Anything *but*," I said. "Clue is our silent partner. She loves to help us solve mysteries."

"But she doesn't love the cold," Ashley said. "That's why we left her in California."

Jade stepped forward. "Well, you girls are in for a treat," she said. "Dakota will be modeling the latest winter fashions this weekend at the Icy Igloo Inn."

"Neat!" Ashley said.

But Dakota didn't look happy. "Mother!" she said. "I told you a gazillion times, I don't want to stay the whole weekend!"

"Sorry, precious. The fashion show is

already set for this Sunday," Jade said.

"Yippee," Dakota muttered.

Ashley and I stared at Dakota. She might be a supermodel, but from what I could see, she had super problems with her mom!

"Now that we're all together," Irving boomed, "how about a tour of the grounds?"

Irving showed us all how to put on shoes that looked like tennis rackets. He said they were snowshoes. Then we followed him past the icy lake.

"All this snow reminds me of my home in Sweden," Lars said with a smile. "I once saw a reindeer in our backyard."

"Did you pet it? Or feed it?" I asked.

Lars shook his head. "I took a picture of it so I would remember every detail," he said. "Then I developed the picture and sculpted a reindeer from a block of ice. It won first prize in the International Chill Challenge!"

"Well, I hate the cold!" Dakota snapped.

"Is it always this freezing around here?"

"Yes, and it's a good thing," Iris said.

"One warm winter the Icy Igloo Inn started melting," Irving explained. "We had to send all the guests home."

As we trekked through the snow, Irving pointed out the sights. "Some of our activities are snowball golf, snowball tennis, snowshoeing—"

"How about snowboarding?" Kevin said. "That's as close to surfing as you can get!"

"Sure!" Irving said. "And you also might enjoy dogsledding."

"Dogsledding!" Jade cried. "Dakota, we can wear our matching furry dogsledding boots with the leather trim again!"

"Give me a break!" Dakota groaned. She turned around and stomped back to the inn.

"Whoa," Kevin said.

Jade turned to the Cathcarts. "I'm sorry about Dakota," she said. "She's just having a little meltdown."

"Meltdown?" Iris repeated.

"D-d-don't even say the word!" Irving stammered.

Ashley and I had to giggle. Irving and Iris had nothing to worry about. It was way below freezing and much too cold for *anything* to melt!

After the tour we went back to the inn and to the bathhouse to freshen up.

At dinner we all sat at the dining room table, which was carved out of ice. While Iris and Irving served yummy cold chicken and potato and macaroni salads, I looked at the other guests. Mr. and Mrs. Douglas were wearing winter coats, but they smelled like coconut sunscreen. Kevin's bulky parka looked bulkier than usual. Jade wasn't eating. She was too busy making sure Dakota didn't drop any food onto her mohair sweater. Brutus nibbled food off Dakota's plate. Lars was sculpting something out of potato salad. A moose, I think.

"Look!" Ashley nodded at her dish. "Even the plates here are made out of ice."

"This is good," Dakota said, "but I wish we could have a hot meal!"

I looked at Kevin to see how he liked the dinner. But then I saw something weird. Kevin's plate looked soggy and wet—as if it was melting!

That's funny, I thought. *No one else's plate is melting.*

"Oh, dear!" Iris's voice interrupted my thoughts. "I forgot to decorate our dinner table with our lovely ice vases."

"I saw your vases earlier," Lars said. "All those great shapes and sizes. They're awesome!"

"I'd like to see them," I said.

"Sure," Irving said. "Let's go." He gave a little smile. "It's not as if your dinner will get cold!"

Ashley and I followed the Cathcarts into the living room.

Iris let out a huge gasp. "My vases!" she cried. "They're gone!"

Iris pointed to a table made of ice. There were bunches of dried flowers on the table—and puddles of frozen water.

I glanced at Ashley. She was staring at the frozen puddles with narrowed eyes.

"I hate to tell you this, Iris," Ashley said. "But I think your vases melted."

That's what I thought too.

"Melted?" Iris cried.

"Impossible!" Irving said. He walked to a thermometer hanging on the wall. "It's twenty-five degrees in here. Nothing ever melts at twenty-five degrees!"

Ashley looked around. "And look—nothing else in this room melted," she said.

"So what are you saying?" Iris asked.

"This was no accident," I said. "Someone melted your vases on purpose!"

Thaw and Order

"How awful!" Iris cried.

"We have to send everyone home!" Irving exclaimed.

"Because of a few melted vases?" Ashley asked.

Irving nodded and said, "What if the person who melted the vases strikes again?"

"And melts the whole inn!" Iris said.

I looked at Ashley, and she looked at me. This was a case for the Trenchcoat Twins!

"Iris, Irving," I said, "what happened

here is a mystery, and we'd like to solve it."

"Are you as good as your great-grandma?" Irving asked.

"Great-grandma Olive taught us everything we know," Ashley said with a grin.

"Then you must be good!" Iris said. "Okay, we could use your help."

First we helped pick up the flowers. Then Ashley and I headed back to the dining room to finish our dinner.

"One of the guests must have heated up those ice vases," Ashley whispered. "Why else would they melt?"

Ashley and I looked at the other guests at the table. I quietly pointed out Kevin's thawing plate to Ashley. Did Kevin have something to do with the puddled vases?

"What's for dessert?" Mr. Douglas called out. "All that swimming made me hungry!"

"Sno-cones!" Irving answered. "We'll have a special Getting to Know You party in the ice-cream parlor!"

"I know everybody already," Dakota said.

"It's a party, Dakota dear!" Jade said excitedly. "And a *party* means party *clothes*!"

Dakota wasn't the only one who dressed up for the party. Ashley and I changed into cool parkas with fake-fur trim. Mine was green. Ashley's was purple.

"What do we know so far about this case?" Ashley asked.

"We know that the vases melted and Kevin's plate thawed today," I said. "We should talk to him first. I also know something else."

"What?" Ashley asked.

I licked my lips and said, "I can't wait to eat some sno-cones!"

We filed into the ice-cream parlor with the others. Music played from a boom box.

"Who's first up for a sno-cone?" Irving called from behind the counter.

“I’ll have one, please,” Dakota said. She carried Brutus over to the counter. “Make mine with lime syrup.”

“One lime sno-cone coming up!” Irving said.

“Stop!” Jade shouted as she ran toward her daughter. “Dakota, what if you drip syrup onto your new parka?”

“But it’s a sno-cone party!” Dakota said.

“Sno-cone, shmoe-cone!” Jade said. She pulled a laptop computer out of her tote bag and shoved it into Dakota’s hands. “Why don’t you show the kids your Dakota Valencia Fashion Files instead?”

“Fashion Files?” Ashley asked.

I was pretty curious too. We watched as Dakota started the computer.

Suddenly an image of Dakota wearing a red and white sundress flashed onto the screen. Dakota kept clicking the mouse. Each time she did, the outfit on the screen changed!

"I have two hundred different outfits on file," Dakota said. "That does not include shoes or accessories."

"Amazing!" Ashley exclaimed. "You can plan all your outfits on your computer!"

Jade ran over to us. She began clicking the mouse by herself. "And if you open this file," she said, "you can watch a video of us in the Mother-Daughter Fashion Show!"

"That's it. I'm out of here," Dakota said. She flipped her hair over her shoulders and stormed out of the parlor.

Jade didn't seem to care. She was too busy admiring herself in the video.

"People *never* think we're mother and daughter," Jade gushed. "They all think we're sisters!"

Across the room Lars was dancing to the music while licking a sno-cone. Kevin was rocking back and forth on a snowboard.

"Cool snowboard, Kevin," I said.

"It's a surfboard, dudes!" Kevin insisted.

"These gnarly waves are totally excellent!"

"What waves?" I whispered.

"I think he's pretending!" Ashley said.

Lars tossed his paper cone into an ice trash can. Then he turned toward the door.

"I'm going to check on my sculptures," Lars said. "I'll be right back."

I turned back to Kevin. "So, how did you like dinner?" I asked. "Those ice dishes were pretty cool."

"Except yours was a bit watery, wasn't it?" Ashley asked.

"Uh, yeah," Kevin said. Suddenly he jumped off his snowboard, tucked it under his arm, and headed out the door.

"Wait! Where are you going?" I asked.

"To get some surfing music, dudes!" Kevin answered. "What's a beach party without surfing tunes?"

"Should we follow him?" Ashley whispered. "What if he's planning to melt something?"

"If he's getting CDs, he'll be back soon,"

I said. "In the meantime let's get some sno-cones while they're hot. I mean . . . cold!"

Ashley and I went to the counter. Irving handed me a sno-cone with cherry syrup. Ashley's had coconut syrup. We didn't know snow could taste so great. But then we noticed that Kevin had not come back yet.

"Let's see what he's up to," I said.

Ashley and I left the parlor. As we passed the sculpture room, I glanced inside. Lars was not there.

Lars said he was going to check on his sculptures, I thought. *I wonder where he is.*

We walked up the hall and called Kevin's name. But as we passed our own room, Ashley stopped, pointed inside, and said, "Mary-Kate, look!"

My eyes popped wide open. The beautiful ice-carved night table in our room had icicles hanging from one corner.

It looked as if it was *melting*!

Howl in the Night

"Our beautiful night table!" Ashley said.

Ashley and I rushed into the room. Not only were there icicles, there was a half-frozen puddle of water underneath.

"We have to tell the Cathcarts," I said.

The sno-cone party was over, so we found Iris and Irving in the living room. When we told them about our night table, they frowned.

"Why would anyone want to melt the Icy Igloo Inn?" Irving cried. He plopped down

onto the ice sofa and . . . *Crack!* It collapsed under him.

"Wha—?" Irving yelped.

"Irv!" Iris shouted. "Are you all right?"

"I—I think so!" Irving said. He looked underneath the sofa and frowned. "The legs of the sofa just cracked!"

"Wow," I said. "Whoever is melting the inn is doing a good job. I mean—a *bad* job!"

Ashley and I inspected the sofa. A half-frozen puddle lay underneath it.

"That does it!" Iris cried. "Irving, we're closing the inn tonight. It's not safe."

"Oh, no!" Ashley cried.

"We were just getting started on this mystery," I said. "Please give us more time."

"But what about the guests?" Irving asked. "We can't have them stay in an inn that's melting."

"We think a guest is doing this," Ashley said. "And we promise to find out which one!"

"Well . . ." Iris started to say.

"I don't know . . ." Irving said.

"Ashley and I always stick to a case until we solve it!" I blurted out.

"Yeah! Great-grandma Olive never quits," Ashley piped up. "And neither do we."

The Cathcarts looked at each other.

"All right, then," Irving said with a nod. "You can have a little more time."

"But hurry!" Iris begged. "Before the Icy Igloo Inn turns into the Slushy Igloo Inn!"

My sister and I went back to our room. Ashley dug into her backpack for her detective notebook. She never goes anywhere without it. We took off our parkas and boots and snuggled under the reindeer skins. When we were nice and warm, we got right to work.

"Let's start with suspects," Ashley said. "We know that Kevin left the party and never came back. But why would he want to melt the Icy Igloo Inn?"

"Kevin doesn't want to stay at the Icy

Igloo Inn," I said. "He wants his parents to take him somewhere warm and beach-y."

Ashley pointed to our partially melted night table. "He was also gone long enough to melt our night table," she said. "And the sofa legs in the living room."

"He didn't have an answer for why his plate was melting too," I added. "That's enough proof for me. Kevin Douglas did it!"

But Ashley shook her head. "Kevin is only a suspect," she said as she wrote his name in her detective notebook. "We can't accuse him of anything until we have—"

"Evidence!" I finished. "I know, I know!"

I also knew that *evidence* was a fancy word for *clues*.

Ashley and I both have strawberry-blond hair and blue eyes. But as detectives Ashley and I are as different as we can be. I like to jump headfirst into a case. Ashley takes her time and searches for every possible clue.

"Okay," I said. "Now that we have suspect number one . . . who *else* might want to melt the Icy Igloo Inn?"

Ashley opened her mouth to say something. But then someone—or something—let out a loud *hooowwwl*!

We ducked under the reindeer skins.

"What was that?" I whispered.

"It sounded as if it came from outside." Ashley gulped. "Maybe it's wolves!"

I tossed off my reindeer skin and ran to the window. The floor felt cold through my socks. I saw the Siberian huskies outside. They were hitched to the dogsled. A figure stood in the sled holding the reins. By the light of the moon I could see who it was. . . .

"It's Lars!" I said.

Ashley peered over my shoulder as Lars shook the reins. He shouted, *"Mush! Mush!"*

The huskies howled again. Then they took off!

"Where is Lars going so late?" Ashley asked in a low voice. "And in the dogsled?"

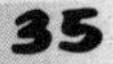

5

UNDERCOVER CLUE

I wondered where Lars could be going too. But then I remembered a few things about him. . . .

"Ashley, do you remember when Lars argued with the Cathcarts?" I asked. "You know, about taking pictures? Maybe he's melting things because he's mad at them."

"He also left the party early. He could have melted the sofa and night table then," Ashley added. "Now he's sneaking away in the middle of the night."

"Maybe he has something to hide," I said. "But what?"

"Let's think of it another way," said Ashley. "What melts ice?"

"Something hot—matches, candles . . ." I said.

"Heaters, electric blankets—" Ashley added.

"What are we waiting for?" I asked. "Let's check out Lars's room for clues before he gets back!"

We slipped back into our parkas and boots. Then we walked quietly to Lars's room. Instead of a door it had a beaded curtain. The beads jingled as we peeked through them.

"Wow!" I said, looking around.

Lars's room looked like a true artist's studio. There were sketches on a small table, and a partially sculpted block of ice on the floor. A stack of art books sat next to a pile of the warmest-looking sweaters.

I wasn't sure it was okay to go into Lars's room.

Suddenly Ashley pointed to something on the floor. "Look, Mary-Kate!" she said. It looked like a pocket-size spray can.

I ran into the room and grabbed it. I read the label: "'Melt-Away Spray. Melts solid ice on contact!'"

"Did you say 'melts ice'?" Ashley asked. "If that's true, we have our evidence."

"I think it's time to write Lars's name in your detective notebook," I said, "as suspect number two!"

"Good morning, girls!" Irving said. "How did you sleep last night?"

Ashley and I walked into the dining room for breakfast. It was Thursday morning. We were ready to start a new day—and ready to look for more clues!

"We slept fine. You were right," I said. "Those reindeer skins were nice and toasty."

Iris rushed in with a plate of muffins. "Did someone say *toast*?" she asked. "No toaster here! Toasters melt ice!"

I looked around the dining room for Lars. *Where did Lars go last night?* I wondered. *And where is he now?*

My thoughts were interrupted by Jade's voice. She was sitting at the table, talking loudly on her cell phone.

"I want Dakota on the cover of *Modern Miss* magazine! Why? Because *I* was on the cover twenty years ago, that's why!"

Jade clicked off her phone. Then she looked up, smiled, and said, "Good morning!"

Dakota strutted in carrying Brutus. She was wearing a yellow coat, black ski pants, and a black furry hat. "I'll have a bowl of cereal," she said. "Brutus will have a bowl of Muttsy Meal."

"Cereal and Muttsy Meal—coming right up!" Irving said as he went to the kitchen.

We all chatted while we ate. Jade did the

most talking. She told us all about Dakota's latest fashion shows in Paris and London.

"That must have been cool!" Ashley said.

"It was way *awful*," Dakota mumbled.

"It *was* awesome, wasn't it?" Jade said over her ringing cell phone. She answered it and began to gab.

The Douglases finished their breakfast. As they stood up, I saw they were dressed in their bathing suits again.

"Ah!" Mr. Douglas said, rubbing his hands together. "It's eleven degrees outside. Great day for a swim!"

Mr. and Mrs. Douglas grabbed their towels and jogged out of the dining room.

Kevin finished eating his blueberry muffin. "Surf City, here I come," he sang.

When breakfast was over, everyone left the room. Ashley and I stayed to help the Cathcarts clear the table. But when I reached for Kevin's dish, I noticed something.

"Kevin's dish is soggy again—as if it's

melting," I pointed out. "And all he ate were two cold muffins."

"Let's take a look at Kevin's room today," Ashley said. "He is still a suspect. Maybe he has something that melts ice too!"

"Do you know where Kevin went?" I whispered.

"Surf's up!" a voice shouted.

We turned and saw Kevin running toward the front door, balancing his snow-board on his head.

Ashley grinned and said, "Does that answer your question?"

We piled the dishes in the kitchen. Then we made our way to Kevin's room.

A reindeer skin lay on the bed, but beach towels were spread out everywhere else. There was also a blowup plastic palm tree in the middle of the room.

"Wow," I said. "The only thing missing here is a clambake!"

Ashley and I searched around the ice

furniture and underneath Kevin's backpack. We didn't find anything suspicious.

"No clues here," I said. "We'd better leave before Kevin decides to come back."

My foot landed on a beach towel as I stepped back.

Crunch!

"What was that?" Ashley asked.

I didn't know. So I bent down and lifted the towel. Underneath were a dozen small bags of potato chips, nacho triangles, and pretzels!

"Look at all this junk food!" I said.

Ashley stared down at the snacks and smiled. "That is not junk, Mary-Kate," she said. "That is *evidence*!"

6

DOWNHILL CHASER

"Evidence?" I cried. "How can chips and pretzels be evidence?"

Ashley smiled as she picked up a crushed bag. "Remember what the Cathcarts said about salt?" she asked. "Salt melts ice. . . ."

"And chips and pretzels are loaded with salt!" I finished. I picked up a bag of pretzels and started to open it.

"Don't eat the evidence!" Ashley said. "I say we save it." She slipped a bag of pretzels into her parka pocket. We covered the other bags back up with the beach towel and left the room.

"Now we have evidence on both Lars and Kevin," I said as we walked down the hall. "But which one is melting the inn?"

Ashley and I decided to question them both. We found Kevin outside, standing at the top of a hill with his snowboard.

"Can we talk to you, Kevin?" I called.

"About what, dudes?" Kevin asked.

Ashley pulled out the pretzel bag. She dangled it in front of Kevin's face and said, "About this, dude."

Kevin gulped. He turned on his board and sped down the hill!

"We can't let him get away!" I said.

"No way am I running down that hill!" Ashley said.

I looked around and saw a sled parked by a tree. "Hop on, Ashley!" I said, grabbing the sled's rope. "We're going for a ride!"

Ashley and I jumped onto the sled. Soon

we were chasing Kevin down the hill! The cold snow blew all around us.

Kevin steadied himself by waving his arms and rocking back and forth. He really did look like a surfer. Until his board flipped over, and he went flying!

"Wipeout!" Kevin shouted before he crashed into a powdery snowdrift.

Our sled came to a stop beside him. Kevin climbed out of the snowdrift and dusted himself off. His cap and sunglasses had been knocked off, but he looked okay.

"Bummer," Kevin said. "I was just about to shoot the curl!"

Ashley held up the pretzel bag. "Okay, Kevin," she said. "What were you doing with salty snacks in your room?"

"Were you using them to melt the inn?" I asked.

"What are you talking about?" Kevin asked. "All I did was sneak in some chips and pretzels to eat. What's the big deal?"

"That's *all* you did with them?" Ashley asked.

Kevin nodded. "I knew the food in this place was worse than my school cafeteria's," he said. "So this time I decided to bring some snacks."

I remembered Kevin's soggy ice dishes. "Did you also sneak them into the dining room?" I asked.

"For sure!" Kevin said. "If I was going to be stuck here a whole week, I was going to make the best of it!"

I didn't know if Kevin was telling the truth. And from the look on Ashley's face, I could tell she didn't either.

"Where did you go the night of the party, Kevin?" Ashley asked. "When you left and didn't come back?"

"I told you. To look for surfer tunes!" Kevin said. His eyes suddenly lit up. "Whoa! Check out those radical breakers. I'm catching a wave!"

Kevin picked up his board. He tucked it under his arm and began running up the hill.

"Does he always have to talk like a surfer?" Ashley groaned.

I laughed. "Let's keep a close eye on him from now on," I said.

Ashley and I dragged the sled up the hill. When we reached the top, I heard a voice shout, "Mary-Kate! Ashley!"

I turned and saw Iris. She was jumping up and down and waving her arms.

"Come quick, girls!" Iris cried. "Something has happened inside the inn. Something terrible!"

7

Hide and Peek

"What happened?" I asked as we ran toward the inn.

Iris didn't say anything. She just whisked us inside and straight to the dining room.

Irving was there, shaking his head. "Look!" he said. The dining room table was lying on its side. Two of its legs had melted away. The legs on four of the chairs had disappeared too!

"Melted!" I gasped.

"The culprit struck again!" Ashley said.

"That does it," Irving declared. "I'm closing the inn before the weekend."

"But the weekend is only two days away!" I said.

"I know we'll solve the case by then," Ashley said. "We already have two suspects."

"All we need to do is stake out the inn," I said. "And we'll catch the culprit in the act." To *stake out* a place means you watch and wait for something to happen.

"But what about our furniture?" Iris asked. She began wringing her hands. "Now that the dining room table is partly melted, where are we going to eat?"

Ashley smiled and said, "I know! How about having a picnic?"

"In the snow?" Irving asked.

"We do everything else in the snow," I said. "So why not a picnic?"

"What a wonderful idea!" Iris said.

"I'll find a picnic basket," Irving said.

"I'll pack up some food," Iris said happily.

As Iris and Irving hurried toward the kitchen, I turned to Ashley. "How can we be at the picnic and stake out the inn at the same time?" I asked.

Ashley snapped her fingers. With her gloves, it wasn't much of a *snap*.

"The video camera!" Ashley said. "I packed our video camera in my duffel bag."

"Right," I said, nodding. "We hide the camera somewhere in the inn, and it does the spying for us!"

"And it has no flash," Ashley added, "so it's not against Icy Igloo Inn rules!"

Our mittens thumped as we high-fived. Then we searched the inn, looking for a good spot to hide the camera.

"How about behind the counter?" I asked in the ice-cream parlor. "It will be well hidden here. And nothing in this room has melted yet, so maybe the culprit will come here next."

"Good idea," Ashley said. "We can switch on the camera right before the picnic."

"Then it's all systems go!" I declared.

Iris and Irving did a great job with the picnic. They brought out thick, furry blankets for us to sit on and a huge picnic basket filled with all kinds of picnic foods.

Ashley and I kept our eyes on Kevin and Lars. Would one of them go inside to melt the inn? If so, our video camera was ready. I just wished we had more video cameras, so we could put one in every room!

"Okay, everybody," Irving said. "Hot dogs are ready!" He took them from a small grill and put them on paper plates for us.

"In two seconds they'll be *cold* dogs," Jade said.

"The hot dogs are pretty good with mustard," Dakota said. She was about to take another bite when Jade gasped.

"Drop it, Dakota!" Jade ordered. "You'll

get mustard all over your cashmere mittens! Here, have a plain hot dog instead. And don't cross your legs. You'll wrinkle your Italian leather ski pants!"

Dakota finished her hot dog—with mustard. Then she stood up. "I think I'll walk Brutus," she said.

Brutus whined as Dakota carried him away. The little Chihuahua didn't seem happy to leave the food.

"Poor Brutus," Ashley murmured.

"Poor Dakota!" I whispered. "Why doesn't Jade give her a break?"

Ashley and I finished our hot dogs and potato salad. Soon we were too stuffed to eat any more. But not too stuffed to challenge each other to a snowball fight!

"You're going down!" I giggled as I packed a snowball between my mittens.

"Oh, yeah?" Ashley said, bobbing and weaving. "Go ahead, make my day!"

We tossed a few snowballs. We stopped

when we saw Kevin get up. He stretched, then began walking toward the inn.

"Where are you going, Kevin?" Mrs. Douglas called.

"To the kitchen," Kevin said over his shoulder, "to look for some ketchup."

I raised my eyebrows at Ashley. *Did Kevin really want ketchup?* I wondered. *Or was he just hungry for trouble?*

I glanced over at Lars next. He was busy building tiny snowmen and snow animals.

"Hey, Lars," I said. "Where did you go in the dogsled last night?"

"Just for a ride," Lars said. "I take the dogsled out all the time, at home. It's fun."

I wasn't sure I believed him. But before I could ask him any more questions, Lars stood up.

"My hat is not warm enough," he said. "I must get my yak-skin earmuffs."

Ashley and I exchanged glances. *Was Lars really cold?* I wondered. *Or was he going inside to turn up the heat on the inn?*

"Surprise, everybody!" Irving called out. He smiled as he picked up a guitar.

"We might not have a campfire going, but we can still sing," Irving said. He propped the guitar on his lap. "Who knows 'Frosty the Snowman'?"

We gathered around Irving. As we sang, Lars came back wearing black earmuffs. Kevin returned with a bottle of ketchup.

While the boys took turns pouring ketchup on cold hot dogs, I leaned over to Ashley and whispered, "Come on. Let's see what the video camera picked up."

Everyone was singing "Dashing through the snow" as Ashley and I left the picnic. We entered the inn and looked around. We saw more partially melted furniture. The ice hat rack in the entrance hall. And the ice bookcase in the library. But when we found melting stools in the ice-cream parlor, we knew what to do!

"Let's check the video camera," I said. "If we're lucky, the culprit is on tape!"

Ashley went behind the counter. She picked up the hidden camera and rewound the tape. Then she pressed PLAY. We both watched the tiny screen on the camera.

"Rats!" I said. "All I can see is the floor!"

"Shh!" Ashley said. "I think I hear something."

I listened closely as the tape played. I could hear something too. It sounded like a whirring noise.

"What is that?" I wondered out loud.

"It sounds like some kind of electric appliance," Ashley said, wrinkling her nose.

"But there are no electrical outlets in this room," I said, looking around. "Or in the whole hotel."

"I know," Ashley said. She stared down as she thought. Suddenly she pointed to the floor near a melting stool. "Mary-Kate, look over there!"

I looked at the frozen puddle under the stool. And I saw something under the clear ice. It was black and triangle-shaped.

I squatted down and examined the object. "It looks like some kind of button."

The ice was still soft. Ashley used the heel of one boot to crack it open. Then she picked up the black object.

"It *is* a button!" Ashley said, turning it around in her hand. "The chunky kind of button that coats and jackets have. And it was *under* the ice. . . ." she said.

"So it must have been dropped here when this puddle was still wet," I added. "That means it has to belong to the culprit!"

"Now we just need to find out whose button it is!" Ashley said.

8

WHO LET THE DOGS OUT?

"Remember," Ashley whispered to me the next morning. "We're looking to see if Lars's or Kevin's jacket buttons match the one we found last night!"

But when Lars and Kevin came for breakfast, they were both wearing parkas with zippers, not buttons!

"Those are the jackets they wore to the picnic last night," Ashley whispered.

"Are you sure?" I whispered back.

"Totally," Ashley said. "Check out the

ketchup stain on the sleeve of Kevin's jacket."

"And Lars's jacket too!" I added. "So who could the button belong to?"

"The latest meltings happened last night during the picnic," Ashley whispered. "Who else left the picnic besides Kevin and Lars?"

"Dakota left early," I reminded her. "Do you think she could be melting the inn?"

"Why would she do it? All Dakota cares about are clothes," Ashley said. "But good detectives would check her out anyway."

We finished our bagels and juice. Then we zipped up our own parkas and hoods and went outside. Big flakes of snow were starting to fall. Ashley and I had fun catching the snowflakes on our tongues. Until we heard Brutus bark.

"Down, Brutus!" We heard Dakota's voice. "Down, boy!"

We found Dakota standing near the freezing lake. The little dog was tugging at his leash and barking at a tree.

"Did Brutus see a squirrel?" I asked.

Dakota shook her head and said, "I think it was a penguin."

I looked at Dakota's coat. It was red with big white buttons. But Dakota wore a different coat every day.

"We found a button in the inn yesterday, Dakota," Ashley said. "Did you lose one?"

"I don't think so," Dakota said. She picked up Brutus. "All my clothes are very well made."

Dakota carried Brutus toward the inn.

"Now what?" I asked as we walked around the grounds. "We still don't know whose button we found."

Iris and Irving were playing volleyball in the snow with Mr. and Mrs. Douglas. Jade stood nearby shouting on her cell phone.

"What do you mean I can't model with Dakota in the fashion show? She's not the only supermodel, you know!"

Nothing looked too fishy. But then we

found some weird-looking footprints. They looked like tennis rackets pressed into the snow.

"Snowshoes!" I said. "We wore those the day we came."

Ashley bent over to inspect the prints. "They're not covered with snow yet," she said. "So they must be fresh. Let's follow them."

The snowshoe prints led to the back of the inn. Then they changed to paw prints. And then sled tracks in the snow.

"The person wearing the snowshoes took out the dogsled," I said.

"Could it be Lars?" Ashley asked. "We saw him take the dogsled out before."

"Maybe now we can find out where he's been going in the dogsled," I said. "Let's follow those tracks and see where they lead."

Trudging through deep snow without snowshoes wasn't easy. But soon we came to the end of the trail. We found the dogsled

tied to a tree. The dogs were there, but the driver was not.

"Hi, guys!" I told the huskies.

"I wish you could talk," Ashley said to the dogs. "So you could tell us who brought you here."

The dogs wagged their gray and white tails as we searched inside the sled. No clues there. But we did find an old, snow-covered cabin nearby. The windows looked grimy. The rusty handle on the door dangled from a single nail.

"It looks pretty creepy," Ashley said.

"I know," I said. "But Lars might be inside."

We walked up to the cabin. I knocked on the door and it swung open—by itself!

Ashley and I peered through the open doorway. It was dark inside, but soon I was able to see a dark figure standing inside.

"There's Lars," I whispered. "What's he doing?"

Lars had his back to us. He was standing next to a wooden table in the middle of the room. On the table were some rectangular pans and a magnifying glass. Several black-and-white photographs were pinned to a clothesline overhead.

"It looks like he's developing pictures," Ashley said quietly. "And they're all of the Icy Igloo Inn."

"Ah!" said Lars suddenly. "I see you discovered my secret!"

9

Lars's Secret

Lars turned around to face us. He had unzipped his parka and something was hanging around his neck.

It was a *camera.*

"Say *ost*!" Lars pointed the lens at us. "That's Swedish for *cheese*!"

I blinked. The flash made me see spots!

"What do you think of my photos?" Lars asked. "Didn't I capture the Icy Igloo Inn perfectly?"

"So *you* took those pictures!" I said.

"I had to!" Lars said. "My next sculpture show will be of a miniature Icy Igloo Inn. So I must remember everything."

"Your next sculpture show?" I repeated.

"I don't get it, Lars," Ashley said. "Why didn't you just tell the Cathcarts *why* you wanted to take pictures?"

"All my sculpture shows are a secret until they're ready," Lars said. "You have no idea how many copycats there are out there!"

That explained why Lars was taking pictures. But I still had questions for him.

"Why did you *really* sneak away in the dogsled the other night?" I asked. "So you could develop your pictures here?"

"Of course. I had to be sneaky," Lars said. "If the Cathcarts saw me taking photos, they'd make me leave the inn." He waved a hand toward the photos. "But as you can see, the flash didn't melt anything!"

Ashley folded her arms across her chest. "The flash might not melt ice," she said.

"But how do you explain the Melt-Away Spray we found in your room?"

Lars's eyes opened wide with surprise. "I use that spray when I sculpt," he said, "to soften the hard edges of the ice."

"You do?" I asked.

"Of course!" Lars said. "How do you think I sculpted a perfect penny?"

But then Lars narrowed his eyes at us. "Why were you snooping around in my room anyway?"

"We had to," Ashley said. "We promised the Cathcarts we'd do our best to find out who was melting the inn."

"Well, it wasn't me!" Lars said. "You won't tell them I was taking pictures, will you?"

"We won't," I said. "But you should."

I glanced at the photos on the clothes-line. "The pictures you took so far are great," I said. "Like that one of Dakota and her mom!"

"Don't remind me of that one!" Lars groaned. "Jade caught me snapping pictures. She told me that if I didn't do a photo shoot of Dakota in all her winter outfits, she'd tell the Cathcarts about my camera!"

Lars gazed at the photo. "That's just *one* of Dakota's outfits," he sighed. "I have about a hundred more to go!"

I stood on tiptoe to get a closer look. Mother and daughter were posed near an ice vanity table in Dakota's room. But something *on* the table really caught my eye.

"Ashley!" I said, still staring. "Do you see what I see in this picture?"

"Where?" Ashley asked.

I pointed to the top of the vanity table and said, "Right there!"

10

Clothes Call

Ashley stood on tiptoe next to me. She squinted as she studied the picture.

"It looks like . . . a hair dryer," Ashley said.

"A hair dryer," I repeated. I thought about the hair dryer Ashley and I used at home. The first thing that popped into my head was the noise it made.

The *whirring* noise!

"The noise we heard on the videotape sounds just like a hair dryer," I said. "Maybe Dakota used a hair dryer to melt the

counter and stools in the ice-cream parlor!"

"Hair dryers aren't allowed in the inn," Lars said. "And why would Dakota want to melt the inn? All she cares about are her clothes. All two hundred sets of them!"

Ashley paced across the room as she thought. "Didn't Dakota tell her mom that she wanted to go home this weekend?" she asked.

"Yeah," I said, nodding. "She seemed really bummed out about it too."

Ashley stopped pacing. "So if the inn started melting, the Cathcarts would shut down the inn," she said. "And send everyone home."

"And Dakota would get her wish!" I exclaimed.

Lars looked confused. "How could Dakota use a hair dryer?" he asked. "There are no electrical outlets in the inn."

Ashley grabbed the magnifying glass and placed it over the picture. "It's a hair dryer

all right," she said. "But I don't see a cord."

"Maybe it's a cordless hair dryer," I said.

Ashley put down the magnifying glass and said, "Whatever it is, we have to go back to the inn and see it for ourselves."

"I'm going with you," Lars said. He zipped his parka over his camera. "Dakota might melt my sculptures next!"

The three of us dashed outside.

"Everybody into the dogsled!" Lars said.

Ashley and I hopped into the sled. Lars stood in the back holding the reins.

"Mush! Mush!" Lars shouted to the dogs.

"Mush?" Ashley repeated.

"It's how you tell the sled dogs to go," Lars said. "I learned it when my parents taught me how to drive a dogsled."

Lars got us back to the inn in just five minutes. Irving was there, putting on snowshoes. Lars handed the reins to him.

"I hope you kids had a nice ride," Irving said.

"Thanks!" Lars said, as we raced toward the front door.

"Yoo-hoo, kids!" Iris called. "We're playing snowball tennis!"

Ashley, Lars, and I turned. Iris was making snowballs while Mr. Cathcart and Kevin whacked them back and forth with rackets.

"I don't see Dakota playing," Ashley said. "Maybe she's in her room."

"Or maybe she's having another 'meltdown'!" I said.

We dashed into the inn and went straight to Dakota's room. Dakota wasn't there. Neither was the hair dryer.

"We have to find that hair dryer!" Ashley said.

I saw Dakota's computer on the vanity table. It was opened to the *Dakota Valencia Fashion Files*.

I put my finger on the mouse and clicked ENTER. The menu popped up on the screen: DRESSES, SKIRTS, PANTS, T-SHIRTS, JACKETS, COATS.

"Coats, huh?" I said to myself.

"What are you doing, Mary-Kate?" Ashley said. "We have to find that hair dryer!"

"We may not be able to find the hair dryer," I said with a smile. "But we might just find the black button!"

Using the mouse, I moved the arrow on the screen to COATS. I clicked. A dozen pictures of Dakota wearing different coats flashed onto the screen.

Ashley and Lars stared over my shoulders at the computer screen.

"She has more clothes than the queen of Sweden!" Lars cried.

Ashley pointed to a red coat. "I'm pretty sure that's the coat Dakota wore yesterday," she said.

"It looks as if it has black buttons," I said, squinting. "But the picture is too tiny to be sure."

"If only I had my magnifying glass." Lars sighed.

"I have one . . . but we don't need it," Ashley said. "Watch this!"

She reached over my shoulder and touched the mouse. Then she moved the little arrow over the coat and clicked. The picture of Dakota wearing the red coat grew bigger and bigger—until it filled up the whole screen!

I studied the buttons. They were big, black, and triangle-shaped.

Ashley dug into the pocket of her parka. She pulled out the button we found and held it next to the screen.

"It's a match!" Ashley declared.

"What does it mean?" Lars asked.

"It means," I said with a smile, "Dakota was at the scene of the crime yesterday!"

Whirrrrrrr!

Ashley and I stared at each other.

"The hair dryer!" Ashley gasped.

"If Dakota is the one melting the inn," I said, "she's at it again!"

11

Model Meltdown!

"We've got to stop her!" Ashley said.

The three of us followed the sound to the ice sculpture room. But we saw a lot more than sculptures!

Dakota was standing in the middle of the room. She was pointing the cordless hair dryer up at the ice chandelier. She was wearing an apple-green snowsuit with a matching hood. Her little dog Brutus was next to her, dressed in an apple-green doggy snowsuit!

"Freeze!" I shouted. "And that's not hard to do in this place!"

Dakota turned off the hair dryer as she whirled around. "I was just drying my hair!" she said.

"With a hood on?" Ashley asked.

"Um . . . er . . ." Dakota stammered as she yanked back the hood. "Hoods help prevent heat damage. It's a supermodel secret!"

"Nice try, Dakota," I said. "But we know you've been melting things in the inn. And now we've caught you at it."

Dakota gulped. Then she stared at us with pleading eyes. "You won't tell, will you?" she said. "I can get you clothes! Lots of clothes! From Paris! And Italy! With totally stylin' hats and accessories!"

"Shoes?" Ashley asked excitedly. "Shoes too?"

"Ashley!" I said. "Snap out of it!" I turned to Dakota. "Sorry, Dakota, but we have to

tell the Cathcarts you were melting the inn."

"I wouldn't do that if I were you!" Dakota said. She spun around and pointed the hair dryer at the ice sculpture of the penny.

"My sculpture!" Lars cried.

"Don't tell the Cathcarts," Dakota warned us. "Or I puddle the penny!"

"No!" Lars cried. "Have a heart! Have a heart!"

But Dakota didn't move the hair dryer.

"Did you know that ice begins to thaw at thirty-two degrees Fahrenheit?" Dakota asked.

Splat!

Dakota shrieked. A big fat drop of water had dripped onto her head!

Splat! Splat! Splat!

More drops! I glanced up. The chandelier that Dakota had started to melt was dripping now—all over Dakota!

"Ew!" Dakota cried. She looked stunned

as she let the hair dryer fall from her hand.

"Dakota, your hair!" a voice cried out. "We spent hours getting it just right, and now you're ruining it!"

I spun around. Jade was rushing into the room. While she covered Dakota's head with her hands, Ashley dove for the hair dryer.

"Got it!" Ashley smiled as she held up the hair dryer.

Just then the Cathcarts marched into the room. "Why, Ashley Olsen!" cried Iris. "Have you been melting our inn?"

12

MESS . . . CONFESS!

"Me?" Ashley squeaked. She looked at the hair dryer in her hand. "Melting the inn?"

"All this time we thought you were trying to help us!" Irving said.

"Ashley, how could you?" Iris wailed.

Ashley opened her mouth to speak, but nothing came out.

So I spoke up for her. "Ashley didn't do it!" I said. "She took the hair dryer away from Dakota."

"Dakota?" Iris and Irving gasped together.

All eyes turned to Dakota. Her mouth was set in a grim line. And her hair was a dripping mess!

"You're making this up!" Jade said. She turned to Dakota. "It's not true, is it? Tell me you weren't melting the inn. Were you?"

Dakota sucked in her breath. She stared at the ground and nodded her drippy head.

"Why on earth would you *do* such a thing?" Jade cried.

"Because I wanted to go home this weekend, Mom!" Dakota said. "So I could go to my cousin Ellen's sleepover tomorrow night!"

Jade wrinkled her nose. "A *sleepover*?" "What's the big deal about a sleepover?"

"It's a big deal for me!" Dakota said. "I've never gone to a sleepover before. All I ever do is work. I want to have fun for a change, like a normal kid!"

Jade stared at her daughter.

I couldn't believe it. I thought everybody

wanted to be like Dakota. But instead, she wanted to be like everybody else!

"I'm so sorry, Dakota," said Jade. She gave her daughter a big hug.

"It's okay, Mom," Dakota said. She turned to face the Cathcarts. "I'm really sorry about what I did to your inn."

Iris and Irving looked at each other. They gave each other a nod.

"We accept your apology," Irving said. "But it won't bring back the things you melted. Like my favorite sofa."

"And my beautiful vases." Iris sighed.

Dakota hung her head. I could tell she felt bad about what she'd done.

"I have an idea," Lars said. "I'll sculpt the things that were melted to replace them!"

"And we'll help!" Ashley suggested.

I smiled at Dakota. "We'll *all* help."

"But I don't know how," Dakota said sadly. "I've never even built a snowman!"

I walked over to Dakota and patted her

shoulder. "If you want to be just like a normal kid," I said, "then building a snowman is a great way to start!"

"And if it's okay with your mom," Ashley said, "maybe we can have our own sleepover tonight!"

"A sleepover?" Dakota squealed. She turned to Jade. "Can we? Can we? Please?"

"Why not?" Jade replied. "You can wear your satin pj's with the matching robe. . . ."

"Mom!" Dakota groaned.

"Yap! Yap!" Brutus barked.

Lars reached down to pet the tiny dog.

Clunk! Lars's camera fell out from under his jacket. The flash went off as it hit the floor!

Brutus scooted under a giant toad ice sculpture.

"Why, Lars Lindstrom!" Iris scolded. "We thought we told you no pictures!"

Lars cleared his throat. "I'm afraid I have to apologize too," he said. "I was taking

pictures of the inn for my next project."

Irving and Iris looked puzzled. "Why?" they asked at the same time.

"I'm sculpting a tiny Icy Igloo Inn," Lars said. He pointed to the floor. "And as you can see, my flash didn't melt a thing!"

"Oh, dear," Iris said, blushing. "I suppose we did overreact just a bit."

"You know, Iris," Irving said, "a sculpture of the Icy Igloo Inn is a fine idea!"

"Yes!" Iris said. "People will see the sculpture and want to visit the real thing!"

The couple grabbed each other's hands.

"Oh, Iris!"

"Oh, Irving!"

"Ahhhh-chooooo!"

Everyone whirled around. The Douglases were walking slowly into the parlor. Mr. Douglas was wrapped in a thick wool blanket. And his nose was flaming red.

"Hey, Dad!" Kevin said. "What's wrong?"

"I caught the worst cold," Mr. Douglas

said, "from swimming in all that ice water."

"We're checking out of this place," Mrs. Douglas said, "and heading for sunny Waikiki Beach . . . in Hawaii!"

Kevin whipped off his sunglasses. He stared at his parents. "All riiiiight!" he shouted. "I mean, cowabunga!"

Everyone laughed.

"Okay!" I said, rubbing my hands together. "If we're going to start building with snow, we'd better put on some gloves."

"If you need extras," Jade said, "Dakota has two hundred pairs!"

Ashley and I headed toward our room.

"I can't believe how great everything turned out," Ashley said. "Dakota is going to her first sleepover, Lars can go on snapping pictures, Kevin will finally get to surf—"

"And we solved another mystery!" I added. "How cool is that?"

"Way cool!" Ashley giggled. "And here at the Icy Igloo Inn, cool rules!"

Hi from both of us,

Ashley and I were visiting our friend Lindsay for the weekend. We were going to watch her compete in the Flower Festival. But someone—or something—was destroying her beautiful tulips, one flower bed at a time. We're on the case, but all the evidence points towards a real live unicorn! Unicorns don't really exist . . . do they?

Could we make sense of the clues, and maybe even catch a unicorn, before all of Lindsay's flowers were destroyed? Want to know what happened? Turn the page for a sneak peek at *The New Adventures of Mary-Kate and Ashley: The Case of the Unicorn Mystery.*

See you next time!

Mary-Kate Olsen

The New Adventures of MARY-KATE & ASHLEY™

A sneak peek at our next mystery…

The Case Of The Unicorn Mystery

"There's someone outside," Ashley whispered. She stared out the window. "In the tulip bed!"

I squinted into the darkness. There was a white figure moving around the flowers.

"Let's go!" Lindsay cried. The three of us hurried out of her bedroom and down the dark stairs.

Lindsay's sister Abby stood by the back door. She was wearing a short pale pink nightgown and her brown hair was messy from sleep.

"Something was in the garden!" Abby said.

"What was it?" Ashley asked.

"I don't know," Abby said. "It ran off."

Lindsay's dad walked across the room, opened the back door, and turned on the outside light. "Oh, no!" he cried.

Everyone crowded around him in the doorway. Lindsay let out a shriek. Her beautiful yellow tulips had been destroyed. Stray petals lay all over the ground. Now Lindsay had only one bed of tulips left for the Flower Festival. She looked like she was about to cry.

Mr. Munro looked around the yard. "There's no one out here anymore." He stepped back into the kitchen and closed the door.

Lindsay sat down heavily at the kitchen table. Abby sat beside her and gave her a hug. She picked up a piece of paper from the table. "Look at this!" she said.

It was the latest issue of *Nick's News*. I

read the headline. "'Unicorn Appears in Town!'"

"A unicorn?" Ashley and Lindsay cried at once.

"It says that a unicorn was spotted yesterday. Several people saw it running through town," I said.

"Do you think there really is a unicorn?" Ashley asked.

"No way," I said.

"But remember what the town legend said? A unicorn will appear after the third rainbow in June. We saw the rainbow yesterday," she said.

"Ashley, there was no unicorn," I insisted.

"There could have been," Abby said. "Several people saw it."

"And don't forget we saw something white in the garden," Lindsay added.

"I think we have another suspect to add to our list," Ashley said. "Maybe a unicorn ate Lindsay's tulips!"

The New Adventures of Mary-Kate and Ashley

"Win a Fun Photo Gift Pack" Sweepstakes

OFFICIAL RULES:

1. **NO PURCHASE OR PAYMENT NECESSARY TO ENTER OR WIN.**
2. **How to Enter.** To enter, complete the official entry form or hand print your name, address, age, and phone number along with the words "*The New Adventures of Mary-Kate and Ashley* Win A Fun Photo Gift Pack Sweepstakes" on a 3" x 5" card and mail to: "*The New Adventures of Mary-Kate and Ashley* Win A Fun Photo Gift Pack Sweepstakes" c/o HarperEntertainment, Attn: Children's Marketing Department, 10 East 53rd Street, New York, NY 10022. Entries must be received no later than June 28, 2005. Enter as often as you wish, but each entry must be mailed separately. One entry per envelope. Partially completed, illegible, or mechanically reproduced entries will not be accepted. Sponsor is not responsible for lost, late, mutilated, illegible, stolen, postage due, incomplete, or misdirected entries. All entries become the property of Dualstar Entertainment Group, LLC, and will not be returned.
3. **Eligibility.** Sweepstakes are open to all legal residents of the United States (excluding Colorado and Rhode Island), who are between the ages of five and fifteen on June 28, 2005 excluding employees and immediate family members of HarperCollins Publishers, Inc., ("HarperCollins"), Parachute Properties and Parachute Press, Inc., and their respective subsidiaries and affiliates, officers, directors, shareholders, employees, agents, attorneys, and other representatives and their immediate families (individually and collectively, "Parachute"), Dualstar Entertainment Group, LLC, and its subsidiaries, affiliates and related companies, officers, directors, shareholders, employees, agents, attorneys, and other representatives and their immediate families (individually and collectively, "Dualstar"), and their respective parent companies, affiliates, subsidiaries, advertising, promotion and fulfillment agencies, and the persons with whom each of the above are domiciled. All applicable federal, state and local laws and regulations apply. Offer void where prohibited or restricted by law.
4. **Odds of Winning.** Odds of winning depend on the total number of entries received. Approximately 250,000 sweepstakes announcements published. All prizes will be awarded. Winners will be randomly drawn on or about July 15, 2005, by HarperCollins, whose decision is final. Potential winners will be notified by mail and will be required to sign and return an affidavit of eligibility and release of liability within 14 days of notification. Prize won by minors will be awarded to parent or legal guardian who must sign and return all required legal documents. By acceptance of the prize, winners consent to the use of their name, photograph, likeness, and biographical information by HarperCollins, Parachute, Dualstar, and for publicity purposes without further compensation except where prohibited.
5. **Grand-Prize.** Five Grand-Prize Winners will win a fun photo gift pack which includes an instant pocket camera (i-Zone from Polaroid), 9 rolls of i-Zone film, a picture frame, photo album, and a signed photograph of Mary-Kate and Ashley. Approximate retail value is $100 per prize.
6. **Prize Limitations.** Prizes are non-transferable and cannot be sold or redeemed for cash. No cash substitute is available. Any federal, state, or local taxes are the responsibility of the winners. Sponsor may substitute prize of equal or greater value, if necessary, due to availability.
7. **Additional terms:** By participating, entrants agree a) to the official rules and decisions of the judges, which will be final in all respects; and to waive any claim to ambiguity of the official rules and b) to release, discharge, and hold harmless HarperCollins, Parachute, Dualstar, and their respective parent companies, affiliates, subsidiaries, employees and representatives and advertising, promotion and fulfillment agencies from and against any and all liability or damages associated with acceptance, use, or misuse of any prize received or participation in any Sweepstakes-related activity or participation in this Sweepstakes.
8. **Dispute Resolution.** Any dispute arising from this Sweepstakes will be determined according to the laws of the State of New York, without reference to its conflict of law principles, and the entrants consent to the personal jurisdiction of the State and Federal courts located in New York County and agree that such courts have exclusive jurisdiction over all such disputes.
9. **Winner Information.** To obtain the name of the winners, please send your request and a self-addressed stamped envelope (residents of Vermont may omit return postage) to "*The New Adventures of Mary-Kate and Ashley* Win A Fun Photo Gift Pack Sweepstakes" Winner, c/o HarperEntertainment, 10 East 53rd Street, New York, NY 10022 after August 15, 2005, but no later than February 15, 2006.
10. **Sweepstakes Sponsor:** HarperCollins Publishers.

BOOKS BOOKS BOOKS BOOKS

so little time

BOOK SERIES

Based on the hit television series

Life is anything but boring for Chloe and Riley Carlson—especially since they've entered high school. Now they're making new friends, meeting new boys, and learning just what being a teenager is all about. No wonder they have so little time!

mary-kate olsen ashley olsen

so little time

the makeover experiment

www.mary-kat

Coming soon wherever books are sold!

Don't miss the other books in the so little time book series!

- ❑ How to Train a Boy
- ❑ Instant Boyfriend
- ❑ Too Good to Be True
- ❑ Just Between Us
- ❑ Tell Me About It
- ❑ Secret Crush
- ❑ Girl Talk
- ❑ The Love Factor
- ❑ Dating Game
- ❑ A Girl's Guide to Guys
- ❑ Boy Crazy
- ❑ Best Friends Forever
- ❑ Love Is in the Air
- ❑ Spring Breakup
- ❑ Get Real
- ❑ Surf Holiday

It's
What
YOU
Read.

Real Books for Real Girls.

mary-kateandashley
fragrances
jasmine spice
juicy peach freesia
mary-kateandashley
Real Scents for Real Girls
www.mary-kateandashley.com
the mary-kateandashley brand
RUGS
Look for the mary-kateandashley brand area rugs at a flooring retailer near you. To find out more, visit www.shawliving.com or call 800-282-7429.
www.mary-kateandashley.com
Shaw Living
DUALSTAR CONSUMER PRODUCTS

Own the Whole Collection!
the mary-kateandashley brand
Mary-Kate Olsen Ashley Olsen
WHEN IN ROME
THE CHALLENGE
Rival sisters.
Challenge of a lifetime.
Let the games begin!
mary-kate olsen ashley olsen
GETTING THERE
mary-kate olsen ashley olsen
HOLIDAY IN THE SUN
Mary-Kate Olsen Ashley Olsen
winning london
OUR LIPS ARE SEALED
SWITCHING GOALS
Passport to Paris
Billboard DAD
HOW THE WEST WAS FUN
DOUBLE, DOUBLE TOIL AND TROUBLE
DUALSTAR VIDEO & DVD
www.mary-kateandashley.com
Distributed by